THE PEABODY HERITAGE

BY

H. P. LOVECRAFT

British Library Cataloguing-in-Publication Data
A catalogue record for this book is available from
the British Library

Contents

H. P. LOVECRAFT

Howard Phillips Lovecraft was born in 1890 in Rhode Island, USA. Although a sickly boy, Lovecraft began writing at a very young age, quickly developing a deep and abiding interest in science. At just sixteen he was writing a monthly astronomy column for his local newspaper. However, in 1908, Lovecraft suffered a nervous breakdown and failed to get into university, sparking a period of five years in which he all but vanished.

In 1913, Lovecraft was invited to join the UAPA (United Amateur Press Association) – a development which re-invigorated his writing. In 1917, he began to focus on fiction, producing such well-known early stories as 'Dagon' and 'A Reminiscence of Dr. Samuel Johnson'. In 1924,

Lovecraft married and moved to New York, but he disliked life there intensely, and struggled to find work. A few years later, penniless and now divorced, he returned to Rhode Island. It was here, during the last decade of his life, that Lovecraft produced the vast majority of his best-known fiction, including 'The Dunwich Horror', 'The Shadow over Innsmouth', 'The Thing on the Doorstep' and arguably his most famous story, 'The Call of Cthulhu'. Having suffered from cancer of the small intestine for more than a year, Lovecraft died in March of 1937.

The Peabody Heritage

H P Lovecraft

I NEVER KNEW my great-grandfather Asaph Peabody, though I was five years old when he died on his great old estate northeast of the town of Wilbraham, Massachusetts. There is a childhood memory of once visiting there, at a time when the old man was lying ill; my father and mother mounted to his bedroom, but I remained below with my nurse, and never saw him. He was reputed to be wealthy, but time whittles away at wealth as at all things, for even stone is mortal, and surely mere money could not be expected to withstand the ravages of the ever-increasing taxation, dwindling a little with each death. And there were many deaths in our family, following my great-grandfather's in 1907. Two of my uncles died after – one was killed on the Western front, and another went down on the *Lusitania*. Since a third uncle had died before them, and none of them had ever married, the estate fell to my father on my grandfather's death in 1919.

My father was not a provincial, though most of his forbears had been. He was little inclined to life in the country, and made no effort to take an interest in the estate he had inherited, beyond spending my great-grandfather's money on various investments in Boston and New York. Nor did my mother share any of my own interest in rural Massachusetts. Yet neither of them would consent to sell it, though on one occasion, when I was home from college, my mother did propose that the property be sold, and my father coldly dismissed the subject; I remember his sudden freezing – there is no more fitting word to describe his reaction – and his curious reference to 'the Peabody heritage' – as well as his carefully phrased words: 'Grandfather predicted that one of his blood would recover the heritage.' My mother had asked scornfully: 'What heritage? Didn't your father just about spend it all?' to which my father made no reply, resting his case in his icy inference that there were certain good reasons why the property could not be sold, as if it were entailed beyond any process of law. Yet he never went near the property; the taxes were paid regularly by one Ahab Hopkins, a lawyer in Wilbraham, who made reports on the property to my parents, though they always ignored them, dismissing any suggestion of 'keeping up' the property by saying it would be like 'throwing good money after bad'.

The property was abandoned, to all intent and purpose; and abandoned it remained. The lawyer had once or twice made a half-hearted attempt to rent it, but even a brief boom in Wilbraham had not brought more than transient renters to the old homestead, and the Peabody place yielded inexorably to time and the weather. It was thus in a sad state of disrepair when I came into the property on the sudden death by motor-car accident of both my parents in the autumn of 1929. Nevertheless, what with the decline in property values which took place subsequent to the inauguration of the depression that year, I determined to sell my Boston property and refurbish the house outside of Wilbraham for my own use. I had enough of a competence on my parents' death so that I could afford to retire from the practice of law, which had always demanded of me greater preciseness and attention than I wished to give to it.

Such a plan, however, could not be implemented until at least part of the old house had been got ready for occupation once more. The dwelling itself was the product of many generations. It had been built originally in 1787, at first as a simple colonial house, with severe lines, an unfinished second storey, and four impressive pillars at the front. But, in time, this had become the basic part of the house, the heart, as it were. Subsequent generations had altered and added to it – at first by the addition of a floating stairway and a second storey; then by various ells and wings, so that at the time I was preparing to make it my residence, it was a large, rambling structure, which occupied over an acre of land, adding to the house itself the lawn and gardens, which were in as great a state of disuse as the house.

The severe colonial lines had been softened by age and less regardful builders, and the architecture was no longer pure, for gambrel roof vied with mansard roof, small-paned windows with large, figured and elaborately sculptured cornices with plain, dormers with unbroken roof. Altogether the impression the old house conveyed was not displeasing, but to anyone of architectural sensibilities, it must have appeared a woeful and unhappy conglomeration of architectural styles and kinds of ornament. Any such impression, however, must surely have been softened by the tremendously spreading ancient elms and oaks which crowded upon the house from all sides save the garden, which had been taken over among the roses, so long grown untended, by young poplar and birch trees. The whole effect of the house, therefore, despite the accretions of time and differing tastes, was of faded magnificence, and even its unpainted walls were in harmony with the great-girthed trees all around.

The house had no less than twenty-seven rooms. Of these, I selected a trio in the south-east corner to be rehabilitated, and all that autumn and early winter, I drove up from Boston to keep an eye on the progress of the venture. Cleaning and waxing the old wood brought out its beautiful colour, installing electricity removed the dark gloom of the rooms, and only the waterworks delayed me until late winter; but by February the twenty-fourth, I was able to take up my residence in the ancestral Peabody home. Then for a month I was occupied with plans for the rest of the house, and, though I had initially thought of having some of the additions torn down and the oldest parts of the structure retained, I soon abandoned this project in favour of the decision to keep the house as it was, for it had a pervasive charm born, no doubt, of the many generations which had lived there, as well as of the essence of the events which had taken place within its walls.

Within that month, I was quite taken with the place, and what had been primarily a temporary move was gladly embraced as a lifelong ideal. But alas, this ideal grew to such proportions that it soon brought about a grandiose departure which subtly altered my direction and threw me off the track on a course I had never wished to take. This scheme was the determination to move to the family vault, which had been cut into a hillside within sight of the house, though away a little from the highway which passed in front of the estate, the remains of my parents, who had been decently interred in a Boston plot. This was in addition to my resolve to make an attempt also to bring back to the United States the bones of my dead uncle, which reposed somewhere in France, and thus re-unite the family, as far as possible, on the ancestral acres near Wilbraham. It was just such a plan as might occur to a bachelor who was also a reclusive solitary, which I had become in the short space of that month, surrounded by the architect's drawings and the lore of the old house which was about to begin a new lease of life in a new era far, far removed from that of its simple beginnings.

It was in pursuit of this plan that I made my way one day in March to the family vault, with the keys the lawyer for the estate had delivered into my hands. The vault was not obtrusive; indeed, no part of it was ordinarily visible except the massive door, for it had been built into a natural slope, and was almost concealed by the trees which had grown without pruning for decades. The door and the vault, as well, had been built to last for centuries; it dated back almost as far as the house, and for many generations every member of the Peabody family from old Jedediah, the first to occupy the house, onward, had been interred here. The door offered me some resistance, since it had not been opened for years, but at length it yielded to my efforts and the vault lay open to me.

The Peabody dead lay in their coffins – thirty-seven of them, some in cubicles, some outside. Some of the cubicles where the earliest Peabodies had lain held only the remains of coffins, while that reserved for Jedediah was completely empty, with not even the dust to show that coffin and body had once reposed in that place. They were in order, however, save for the casket which bore the body of my great-grandfather Asaph Peabody; this seemed curiously disturbed, standing out of line with the others, among those more recent ones – my grandfather's and my one uncle's – which had no cubicles of their own but were simply on a ledge extended outward from the cubicled wall. Moreover, it seemed as if someone had lifted or attempted to lift the cover, for one of the hinges was broken, and the other loosened.

My attempt to straighten my great-grandfather's coffin was instinctive, but in so doing the cover was still further jostled and slipped partially off, revealing to my startled gaze all that remained of Asaph Peabody. I saw that through some hideous error, he had been buried face downward – I did not want to think, even at so long a time after his death, that the old man might have been buried in a cataleptic state and so suffered a painful death in that cramped, airless space. Nothing but bones survived, bones and portions of his garments. Nevertheless, I was constrained to alter mistake or accident, whichever it might be; so I removed the cover of the coffin, and reverently turned skull and bones over so that the skeleton of my great-grand-father lay in its rightful position. This act, which might have seemed grisly in other circumstances, seemed only wholly natural, for the vault was aglow with the sunlight and shadows that speckled the floor through the open door, and it was not at that hour a cheerless place. But I had come, after all, to ascertain how much room remained in the vault, and I was gratified to note that there was ample room for both my parents, my uncle – if his remains could be found and brought thither from France – and, finally, myself.

I prepared, therefore, to carry on with my plans, left the vault well locked behind me, and returned to the house pondering ways and means of bringing my uncle's remains back to the country of his birth. Without delay, I wrote to the authorities in Boston on behalf of the disinterment of my parents, and to those of the county in which I now resided for permission to re-inter my parents in the family vault.

The singular chain of events which seemed to centre about the old Peabody homestead began, as nearly as I can recall, on that very night. True, I had had an oblique kind of warning that something might be amiss with the old house, for old Hopkins, on surrendering his keys, had asked me insistently when I came to take possession whether I was sure I wanted to take this step, and had seemed equally intent upon pointing out that the house was 'a lonely sort of place', that the farming neighbours 'never looked kindly on the Peabodys', and that there had always been a 'kind of difficulty keeping renters there'. It was one of those places, he said, almost with relish at making a distinct point, 'to which nobody ever goes for a picnic. You'll never find paper plates or napkins *there!*' – a plethora of ambiguities which nothing could persuade the old man to reduce to facts, since, evidently, there were no facts, but that the neighbours frowned upon an estate of such magnitude in the midst of what was otherwise good farming land. This, in truth, stretched out on all sides of my property of but forty acres, most of it woods – a land of neat fields, stone walls, rail fences, along which trees grew and shrubbery made adequate cover for birds. An old man's talk, I thought it, given rise by his kinship with the farmers who surrounded me: solid, sturdy Yankee stock, no whit different from the Peabodys, save that they toiled harder and perhaps longer.

But on that night, one on which the winds of March howled and sang among the trees about the house, I became obsessed with the idea that I was not alone in the house. There was a sound not so much of footsteps as of *movement* from somewhere upstairs, one that defies description, save that it was as of someone moving about in a narrow space, forward and back, forward and back. I remember that I went out in the great dark space into which the floating stairway descended, and listened to the darkness above; for the sound seemed to drift down the stairs, sometimes unmistakable, sometimes a mere whisper; and I stood there listening, listening, listening, trying to identify its source, trying to conjure up from my rationalisation some explanation for it, since I had not heard it before, and concluded at last that in some fashion a limb of a tree must be driven by the wind to brush against the house, forward and back. Settled on this, I returned to my quarters, and was no more disturbed by it – not that it ceased, for it did not, but that I had given it a rational excuse for existence.

I was less able to rationalise my dreams that night. Though ordinarily not at all given to dreams, I was literally beset by the most grotesque phantasms of sleep, in which I played a passive role and was subjected to all manner of distortions of time and space, sensory illusions, and several frightening glimpses of a shadowy figure in a conical black hat with an equally shadowy creature at his side. These I saw as through a glass, darkly, and the twilit landscape as through a prism. Indeed, I suffered not so much dreams as fragments of dreams, none of them having either beginning or ending, but inviting me into an utterly bizarre and alien world, as through another dimension of which I was not aware in the mundane world beyond sleep. But I survived that restless night, if somewhat haggardly.

On the very next day I learned a most interesting fact from the architect who came out to discuss my plans for further renovation, a young man not given to the quaint beliefs about old houses common to isolated, rural areas. 'One who came to look at the house would never think,' he said, 'that it had a secret room – well hidden – would you?' he said, spreading his drawings before me.

'And has it?' I asked.

'Perhaps a "priest's hole",' he guessed. 'For runaway slaves.'

'I've never seen it.'

'Nor I. But look here . . .' And he showed me on the plans he had reconstructed from the foundations and the rooms as we knew them, that there was a space unaccounted for along the north wall upstairs, in the oldest part of the house. No priest's hole, certainly; there were no Papists among the Peabodys. But runaway slaves – perhaps. If so, however, how came it there so early, before there were enough slaves to make the run for Canada to justify the room's coming into being? No, not that either.

'Can you find it, do you think?' I asked.

'It has to be there.'

And so indeed it was. Cleverly concealed, though the absence of a window in the north wall of the bedroom ought to have warranted an earlier examination. The door to it was hidden in the finely-wrought carvings which decorated that entire wall, which was of red cedar; had one not known the room must have been there, one would hardly have seen the door which had no knob and worked only by pressure upon one of the carvings, which the architect found, not I, for I have never had an adeptness at things of that kind. However it lay rather within the province of an architect than my own and I paused only long enough to study the rusty mechanism of the door before stepping into the room.

It was a small confining space. Yet it was not as small as a priest's hole; a man could walk upright in it for a distance of ten feet or so, though the slant of the roof would cut off any walking in the direction opposed to it. The long way, yes; across to the wall, no. What was more, the room bore every sign of having been occupied in past time, for it was left undisturbed, there were still books and papers about, as well as chairs which had been used at a small desk against one wall.

The room presented the most singular appearance. Though it was small, its angles seemed to be awry, as if the builder were subtly determined to confound its owner. Moreover, there were curious designs drawn upon the floor, some of them actually cut into the planking in a crudely barbarous fashion, roughly circular in plan, with all manner of oddly repellent drawings around the outer and inner edges. There was a similar repulsiveness about the desk, for it was black, rather than brown, and it had the surprising appearance of having been burned; it looked, indeed, as if it served in more than the capacity of a desk. On it, moreover, was a stack of what looked at first glance to be very ancient books, bound in some sort of leather, as well as a manuscript of some kind, likewise bound.

There was little time for any examination, however, for the

architect was with me and, having seen all he wished, which was just sufficient to verify his suspicion of the room's existence, he was eager to be off.

'Shall we plan to eliminate it, cut in a window?' he asked, and added, 'Of course, you won't want to keep it.'

'I don't know,' I answered. 'I'm not sure. It depends on how old it is.'

If the room were as ancient as I thought it to be, then I would be quite naturally hesitant to destroy it. I wanted a chance to poke around it a little, to examine the old books. Besides, there was no haste; this decision did not need to be made at once; there were other things the architect could do before either of us need think about the hidden room upstairs. It was there that the matter rested.

I had fully intended to return to the room next day, but certain events intervened. In the first place, I spent another very troubled night, the victim of recurrent dreams of a most disturbing nature, for which I could not account, since I had never been given to dreams except as a concomitant of illness. These dreams were, perhaps not unnaturally, of my ancestors, particularly of one long-bearded old fellow, wearing a conical black hat of strange design, whose face, unfamiliar to me in dream, was in actuality that of my great-grandfather Asaph, as a row of family portraits in the lower hall verified next morning. This ancestor seemed to be involved in an extraordinary progression through the air, quite as if he were flying. I saw him walking through walls, walking on the air, silhouetted among treetops. And wherever he went, he was accompanied by a large black cat which had the same ability to transcend the laws of time and space. Nor did my dreams have any progression or even, each within itself, any unity; they were a mixed-up sequence of scenes in which my great-grandfather, his cat, his house, and his property took part as in unrelated tableaux. They were distinctly related to my dreams of the previous night, and accompanied again by all the extra-dimensional trappings of those first nocturnal experiences, differing only in that they possessed greater clarity. These dreams insistently disturbed me throughout the night.

I was thus in no mood to learn from the architect that there would be some further delay in the resumption of work at the Peabody place. He seemed reticent or reluctant to explain, but I pressed him to do so, until at last he admitted that the workmen he had hired had all notified him early this morning that none of them wished to work on this 'job'. Nevertheless, he assured me, he would have no difficulty hiring some inexpensive Polish or Italian labourers from Boston, if I would be a little patient with him. I had no alternative, but, in fact, I was not as much annoyed as I pretended to be, for I began to have certain doubts about the wisdom of making all the alterations I had intended. After all, a part of the old house must necessarily stand with no more than re-inforcement, for much of the charm of the old place lay in its age; I adjured him, therefore, to take his time, and went out to make such purchases as I had intended to make when I came into Wilbraham.

I had hardly begun to do so before I was aware of a most sullen attitude on the part of the natives. Whereas, heretofore, they had either paid me no attention at all, since many of them did not know me, or they had greeted me perfunctorily, if they had made my acquaintance, I found them on that morning of one mind – no one wished to speak to me or to be seen speaking to me. Even the storekeepers were unnecessarily short, if not downright unpleasant, their manner suggesting plainly that they would appreciate my taking my trade elsewhere. It was possible, I reflected, that they had learned of my plans to renovate the old Peabody house, and might be opposed to it on twin grounds – either that the renovation would contribute to the destruction of its charm, or that it would, on the other hand, give another and longer lease of life to a piece of property that surrounding farmers would much have preferred to cultivate, once the house and the woods were gone.

My first thoughts, however, soon gave way to indignation. I was not a pariah, and I did not deserve to be shunned like one, and when, finally, I stopped in at the office of Ahab Hopkins, I unburdened myself to him rather more volubly than was my custom, even though, as I could see, I made him uneasy.

'Ah, well, Mr Peabody,' he said, seeking to soothe my ruffled composure, 'I would not take that too seriously. After all, these people have had a grievous shock, and they are in an ugly, suspicious mood. Besides, they are basically a superstitious lot. I am an old man, and I have never known them to be otherwise.'

Hopkins's gravity gave me pause. 'A shock, you say. You must forgive me – I've heard nothing.'

He favoured me with a most curious look, at which I was quite taken aback. 'Mr Peabody, two miles up the road from your place lives a family by the name of Taylor. I know George well. They have ten children. Or perhaps I had better say "had". Last night, their second youngest, a child of slightly over two years of age, was taken from his bed and carried off without a trace.'

'I am sorry to hear it. But what has that got to do with me?'

'Nothing, I'm sure, Mr Peabody. But you're a comparative stranger here, and, well – you must know it sooner or later – the name of Peabody is not looked on with pleasure – in fact, I may say it is hated – by many people of the community.'

I was astounded and did not attempt to hide it. 'But why?'

'Because there are many people who believe every kind of gossip and muttered talk, no matter how ridiculous it is,' Hopkins answered. 'You are an old enough man to realise that it is so, even if you're unfamiliar with our rural countryside, Mr Peabody. There were all manner of stories common about your great-grandfather, when I was a child, and, since during the years of his incumbency of the homestead, there were certain ugly disappearances of little children, of whom no trace was ever found, there is possibly a natural inclination to connect these two events – a new Peabody on the homestead, and a recurrence of a kind of event associated with another Peabody's residence there.'

'Monstrous!' I cried.

'Undoubtedly,' Hopkins agreed with an almost perverse amiability, 'but so it is. Besides, it is now April. Walpurgis Night is scarce a month away.'

I fear my face must have been so blank as to disconcert him.

'Oh, come, Mr Peabody,' said Hopkins with false joviality, 'you are surely aware that your great-grandfather was considered to be a warlock!'

I took my leave of him, gravely disturbed. Despite my shock and outrage, despite my indignation at the manner in which the natives showed their scorn and – yes, fear – of me, I was even more upset by the nagging suspicion that there was a disquieting logic to the events of the previous night and this day. I had dreamed of my great-grandfather in strange terms indeed, and now I heard him spoken of in far more significant terms. I knew only enough to know that the natives had looked upon my great-grandfather superstitiously as the male counterpart of a witch – a warlock or wizard; by whatever name they called him, so they had seen him. I made no further attempt to be even decently courteous to the natives who turned their heads when I came walking toward them, but got into my car and drove out to the homestead. There my patience was still further tried, for I found nailed to my front door a crude warning – a sheet of tablet paper upon which some illiterate, ill-intentioned neighbour had scrawled in pencil: '*Git out – or els.*'

Possibly because of these distressing events, my sleep that night was far more troubled by dreams than it had been on previous nights. Save for one major difference – there was more continuity in the scenes I saw while I tossed in restless slumber. Again it was my great-grandfather, Asaph Peabody, who occupied them, but he seemed now to have grown so sinister in appearance as to be threatening, and his cat moved with him with the hair of its neck ruffled, its pointed ears forward, and tail erect – a monstrous creature, which glided or floated along beside or behind him. He carried something – something white, or flesh-coloured, but in the murkiness of my dream would not permit me to recognise it. He went through woods, over countryside, among trees; he travelled in narrow passageways, and once, I was certain, he was in a tomb or vault. I recognised, too, certain parts of the house. But he was not alone in his dreams – lingering always in the background was a shadowy, but monstrous Black Man – not a Negro, but a man of such vivid blackness as to be literally darker than night, but with flaming eyes which seemed to be of living fire. There were all manner of lesser creatures about the old man – bats, rats, hideous little beings which were half human, half rat. Moreover, I was given to auditory hallucinations simultaneously, for from time to time, I seemed to hear muffled crying, as if a child were in pain, and, at the same time, a hideous, cackling laughter, and a chanting voice saying: 'Asaph will *be* again. Asaph will *grow* again.'

Indeed, when at last I woke from this continuing nightmare, just as the dawn light was making itself manifest in the room, I could have sworn that the crying of a child still sounded in my ears, as if it came from within the very walls itself. I did not sleep again, but lay wide-eyed, wondering what the coming night would bring, and the next, and the next after that.

The coming of the Polish workmen from Boston put my dreams temporarily from my mind. They were a stolid, quiet lot. Their foreman, a thick-set man named Jon Cieciorka, was matter-of-fact and dictatorial with the men under him; he was a well-muscled fellow of fifty or thereabouts, and the three men whom he directed moved in haste at his command, as if they feared his wrath. They had told the architect that they could not come for a week, the foreman explained, but another job had been postponed, and here they were; they had driven up from Boston after sending the architect a telegram. But they had his plans, and they knew what must be done.

Their very first act was to remove the plaster from the north wall of the room immediately beneath the hidden room. They had to work carefully, for the studding which supported the second storey could not be disturbed, nor need it be. Plaster and lathing, which, I saw as they began, was of that old-fashioned kind made by hand, had to be taken off and replaced; the plaster had begun to discolour and to break loose years before, so that the room was scarcely habitable. It had been so, too, with that corner of the house which I now occupied, but, since I had made greater changes there, the alterations had taken longer.

I watched the men work for a little while, and had just become accustomed to the sounds of their pounding, when suddenly, they ceased. I waited a moment, and then started up and went out into the hall. I was just in time to see all four of them, clustered near the wall, cross themselves superstitiously, back away a little, and then break and run from the house. Passing me, Cieciorka flung an epithet at me in horror and anger. Then they were out of the house, and while I stood as if rooted to the spot, I heard their car start and leap away from my property.

Utterly bewildered, I turned towards where they had been working. They had removed a considerable section of the plaster and lathing; indeed, several of their tools were still scattered about. In their work, they had exposed that section of the wall which lay behind the baseboard, and all the accumulated detritus of the years which had come to rest in that place. It was not until I drew close to the wall that I saw what they must have seen and understood what had sent these superstitious louts running in fear and loathing from the house.

For at the base of the wall, behind the baseboard, there lay, among long yellowed papers half gnawed away by mice, yet still bearing on their surfaces the unmistakably cabalistic designs of some bygone day, among wicked implements of death and destruction – short, dagger-like knives rusted by what must surely have been blood – *the small skulls and bones of at least three children!*

I stared unbelievingly, for the superstitious nonsense I had heard only a day before from Ahab Hopkins now took on a more sinister cast. So much I realised on the instant. Children had disappeared during my great-grandfather's aegis; he had been suspected of wizardry, of witchcraft, of playing roles in which the sacrifice of little children was an integral part; now here, within the walls of his house, were such remains as lent weight to the native suspicions of his nefarious activities!

Once my initial shock had passed, I knew I must act with despatch. If this discovery were made known, then indeed my tenure here would be bitterly unhappy, made so by the god-fearing natives of the neighbourhood. Without hesitating further, I ran for a cardboard box and, returning to the wall with it, gathered up every vestige of bone I could find, and carried this gruesome burden to the family vault, where I emptied the bones into the cubicle which had once held the remains of Jedediah Peabody, now long since gone to dust. Fortunately, the small skulls disintegrated, so that anyone searching there would find only the remains of someone long dead, and only an expert would have been able to determine the origin of the bones which remained sufficiently unimpaired to offer any key. By the time any report from the Polish workmen came back to the architect, I would be able to deny the truth of them, though for this report I was destined to wait in vain, for the fear-ridden Poles never revealed to the architect a word of their real reason for deserting their job.

I did not wait to learn this from the architect, who was bound eventually to find someone who would undertake such alteration as I wished made, but guided by an instinct I did not know I possessed, I made my way to the hidden room, carrying a powerful flashlight, determined to subject it to the most painstaking examination. Almost at once upon entering it, however, I made a spine-chilling discovery; though the marks the architect and I had made in our brief foray into the room were still identifiably evident, there were other, more recent marks which suggested that someone – or something – had been in this room since I had last entered it. The marks were plain to be seen – of a man, bare of foot, and, equally unmistakably, the prints of a cat. But these were not the most terrifying evidences of some sinister occupation – they began out of the north-east corner of the curiously angled room, at a point where it was impossible for a man to stand, and scarcely high enough for a cat; yet it was here that they materialised in the room, and from this point that they came forward, proceeding in the direction of the black desk – where there was something far worse, though I did not notice it until I was almost upon the desk in following the footsteps.

The desk had been freshly stained. A small pool of some viscous fluid lay there, as if it had boiled up out of the wood – scarcely more than three inches in diameter, next to a mark in the dust as if the cat or a doll or a bundle of some kind had lain there. I stared at it, trying to determine what it might be in the glow of my flashlight, sending my light ceiling-ward to detect, if possible, any opening through which rain might have come, until I remembered that there had been no rainfall since my first and only visit to this strange secret room. Then I touched my index finger to the pool and held it in the light. The colour was red – the colour of blood – and simultaneously I knew without being told that this was what it was. Of how it came there I dared not think.

By this time the most terrifying conclusions were crowding to mind, but without any logic. I backed away from the desk, pausing only long enough to snatch up some of the leather-bound books, and the manuscript which reposed there; and with these in my possession, I retreated from the room into the more prosaic surroundings outside – where the rooms were not constructed of seemingly impossible angles, suggesting dimensions beyond the knowledge of mankind. I hastened almost guiltily to my quarters below, hugging the books carefully to my bosom.

Curiously, as soon as I opened the books, I had an uncanny conviction that I knew their contents. Yet I had never seen them before, nor, to the best of my knowledge, had I ever encountered such titles as *Malleus Maleficarum* and the *Daemonialitas* of Sinistrari. They dealt with witch-lore and wizardry, with all manner of spells and legends, with the destruction of witches and warlocks by fire, with their methods of travel – 'Among their chief operations are being bodily transported from place to place . . . seduced by the illusions and phantasms of devils, do actually, as they believe and profess, ride in the night-time on certain beasts . . . or simply walk upon the air out of the openings built for them and for none other. Satan himself deludes in dreams the mind which he holds captive, leading it through devious ways. . . . They take the unguent, which they made at the devil's instruction from the limbs of children, particularly of those whom they have killed, and anoint with it a chair or a broomstick; whereupon they are immediately carried up into the air, either by day or by night, and either visibly or, if they wish, invisibly . . .' But I read no more of this, and turned to Sinistrari.

Almost at once my eye fell upon this disturbing passage – '*Promittunt Diabolo statis temporibus sacrificia, et oblationes; singulis quindecim diebus, vel singulo mense saltem, necem alicujus infantis, aut mortale veneficium, et singulis hebdomadis alia mala in damnum humani generis, ut grandines, tempestates, incendia, mortem animalium . . .*' setting forth how warlocks and witches must bring about, at stated intervals, the murder of a child, or some other homicidal act of sorcery, the mere reading of which filled me with an indescribable sense of alarm, as a result of which I did no more than glance at the other books I had brought down, the *Vitae sophistrarum* of Eunapius, Anania's *De Natura Daemonum*, Stampa's *Fuga Satanae*, Bouget's *Discours des Sorciers*, and that untitled work by Olaus Magnus, bound in a smooth black leather, which only later I realised was human skin.

The mere possession of these books betokened a more than ordinary interest in the lore of witchcraft and wizardry; indeed, it was such manifest explanation for the superstitious beliefs about my great-grandfather which abounded in and about Wilbraham, that I understood at once why they should have persisted for so long. Yet there must have been something more, for few people could have known about these books. What more? The bones in the wall beneath the hidden chamber spoke damningly for some hideous connection between the Peabody house and the unsolved crimes of other years. Even so, this was surely not a public one. There must have been some overt feature of my great-grandfather's life which established the connection in their minds, other than his reclusiveness and his reputation for parsimony, of which I knew. There was not likely to be any key to the riddle among these things from the hidden room, but there might well be some clue in the files of the Wilbraham *Gazette*, which were available in the public library.

Accordingly, half an hour later found me in the stacks of that institution, searching through the back issues of the *Gazette*. This was a time-consuming effort, since it involved a blind search of issue after issue during the later years of my great-grandfather's life, and not at all certain to be rewarding, though the newspapers of his day were less hampered and bound by legal restrictions than those of my own time. I searched for over an hour without coming upon a single reference to Asaph Peabody, though I did pause to read accounts of the 'outrages' perpetrated upon people – primarily children – of the countryside in the vicinity of the Peabody place, invariably accompanied by editorial queries about the 'animal' which was 'said to be a large black creature of some kind, and it has been reported to be of different sizes – sometimes as large as a cat, and sometimes as big as a lion' – which was a circumstance no doubt due solely to the imagination of the reporting witnesses, who were principally children under ten, victims of mauling or biting, from which they had made their escape, happily more fortunate in this than younger children who had vanished without trace at intervals during the year in which I read: 1905. But throughout all this, there was no mention of my great-grandfather; and, indeed, there was nothing until the year of his death.

Then, and only then, did the editor of the *Gazette* put into print what must have represented the current belief about Asaph Peabody. 'Asaph Peabody is gone. He will long be remembered. There are those among us who have attributed to him powers which belonged rather more to an era in the past than to our own time. There was a Peabody among those charged at Salem; indeed, it was from Salem that Jedediah Peabody removed when he came to build his home near Wilbraham. The pattern of superstition knows no reason. It is perhaps mere coincidence that Asaph Peabody's old black cat has not been seen since his death, and it is undoubtedly mere ugly rumour that the Peabody coffin was not opened before interment because there was some alteration in the body tissues or in the conventions of burial to make such opening unwise. This is again lending credence to old wives' tales – that a warlock must be buried face downward and never thereafter disturbed, save by fire. . . .'

This was a strange, oblique method of writing. Yet it told me much, perhaps uncomfortably more than I had anticipated. My great-grandfather's cat had been looked upon as his familiar – for every witch or warlock has his personal devil in any shape it might care to assume. What more natural than my great-grandfather's cat should be mistaken for his familiar, for it had evidently in life been as constant a companion to him as it was in my dreams of the old man? The one disturbing note struck by the editorial comment lay in the reference to his interment, for I knew what the editor could have not have known – that Asaph Peabody had indeed been buried face downward. I knew more – that he had been disturbed, and should not have been. And I suspected yet more – that something other than myself walked at the old Peabody homestead, walking in my dreams and over the countryside and in the air!

That night, once more, the dreams came, accompanied by that same exaggerated sense of hearing, which made it seem as if I were attuned to cacophonous sound from other dimensions. Once again my great-grandfather went about his hideous busi- ness, but this time it seemed that his familiar, the cat, stopped several times and turned to face squarely at me, with a wickedly triumphant grin on its evil face. I saw the old man in a conical black hat and a long black robe walking from woodland seem- ingly through the wall of a house, coming forth into a darkened room, spare of furnishings, appearing then before a black altar, where the Black Man stood waiting for the sacrifice which was too horrible to watch, yet I had no alternative, for the power of my dreams was such that I must look upon this hellish deed. And I saw him and his cat and the Black Man again, this time in the midst of a deep forest, far from Wilbraham, together with many others, before a large outdoors altar, to celebrate the Black Mass and the orgies that followed upon it. But they were not always so clear; sometimes the dreams were only arrow- swift descents through unlimited chasms of strangely coloured twilight and bafflingly cacophonous sound, where gravity had no meaning, chasms utterly alien to nature, but in which I was always singularly perceptive on an extra-sensory plane, able to hear and see things I would never have been aware of while waking. Thus I heard the eldritch chants of the Black Mass, the screams of a dying child, the discordant music of pipes, the inverted prayers of homage, the orgiastic cries of celebrants, though I could not always see them. And on occasion, too, my dreams conveyed portions of conversations, snatches of words, meaningless of themselves, but capable of dark and disquieting explication.

'Shall he be chosen?'

'By Belial, by Beelzebub, by Sathanus . . .

'Of the blood of Jedediah, of the blood of Asaph, companioned by Balor.'

'Bring him to the Book!'

Then there were those curious figments of dreams in which I myself appeared to be taking part, particularly one in which I was being led, alternately by my great-grandfather and by the cat, to a great black-bound book in which were written names in glowing fire, countersigned in blood, and which I was instructed to sign, my great-grandfather guiding my hand, while the cat, whom I heard Asaph Peabody call Balor, having clawed at my wrist to produce blood into which to dip the pen, capered and danced about. There was about this dream one aspect which had a more disturbing bond to reality. In the course of the way through the woods to the meeting place of the coven, the path led beside a marsh where we walked in the black mud of the sedge, near to foetid slough in a place where there was a charnel odour of decay; I sank into the mud repeatedly in that place, though neither the cat nor great-grandfather seemed to more than float upon its surface.

And in the morning, when at last I awoke after sleeping over long, I found upon my shoes, which had been clean when I went to bed, a drying black mud which was the substance of my dream. I started from bed at the sight of them, and followed the tracks they had made easily enough, tracing them backwards, out of the room, up the stairs, into the hidden room on the second storey – and, once there, inexorably, to that same bewitched corner of peculiar angle from which the footprints in the dust had led into the room! I stared in disbelief, yet my eyes did not deceive me. This was madness, but it could not be denied. Nor could the scratch on my wrist be wished out of existence.

I literally reeled from the hidden room, beginning at last vaguely to understand why my parents had been loath to sell the Peabody homestead; something had come down to them of its lore from my grandfather, for it must have been he who had had great-grandfather buried with his face downward in the family crypt. And, however much they may have scorned the superstitious lore they had inherited, they were unwilling to chance its defiance. I understood, too, why periods of rental had failed, for the house itself was a sort of focal point for forces beyond the comprehension or control of any one person, if indeed any human being; and I knew that I was already infected with the aura of the habitation, that, indeed, in a sense I was a prisoner of the house and its evil history.

I now sought the only avenue of further information open to me. The manuscript of the journal kept by my great-grandfather. I hastened to it directly, without pausing for breakfast, and found it to be a sequence of notes, set down in his flowing script, together with clippings from letters, newspapers, magazines, and even books, which had seemed to him pertinent, though these were peculiarly unconnected, yet all dealing with inexplicable events – doubtless, in great-grandfather's eyes, sharing a common origin in witchcraft. His own notes were spare, yet revealing.

'Did what had to be done today. J taking on flesh, incredibly. But this is part of the lore. Once turned over, all begins again. The familiar returns, and the clay takes shape again a little more with each sacrifice. To turn him back would be futile now. There is only the fire.'

And again:

'Something in the house. A cat? I see him, but cannot catch him.'

'Definitely a black cat. Where he came from, I do not know. Disturbing dreams. Twice at a Black Mass.'

'In dream the cat led me to the Black Book. Signed.'

'In dream an imp called Balor. A handsome fellow. Explained the bondage.'

And soon after:

'Balor came to me today. I would not have guessed him the same. He is as handsome a cat as he was a young imp. I asked him whether this was the same form in which he had served J. He indicated that it was. Led the way to the corner with a strange and extra-dimensional angle which is the door to outside. J had so constructed it. Showed me how to walk through it . . .'

I could bear to read no further. Already I had read far too much.

I knew now what had happened to the remains of Jedediah Peabody. And I knew what I must do. However fearful I was of what I must find, I went without delay to the Peabody crypt, entered it, and forced myself to go to the coffin of my great-grandfather. There, for the first time, I noticed the bronze plate attached beneath the name of Asaph Peabody, and the engraving upon it: 'Woe betide him who disturbs his rest!'

Then I raised the lid.

Though I had every reason to expect what I saw, I was horrified no less. For the bones I had last seen were terribly altered. What had been but bone and fragments, dust and tatters of clothing, had begun a shocking alteration. Flesh was beginning to grow once again on the remains of my great-grandfather, Asaph Peabody – flesh that took its origin from the evil upon which he had begun to live anew when I had so witlessly turned over his mortal remains – and from that other thing within his coffin – the poor, shrivelling body of that child which, though it had vanished from the home of George Taylor less than ten days ago, already had a leathern, parchment appearance, as if it were drained of all substance, and partially mummified!

I fled the vault, numb with horror, but only to build the pyre I knew I must gather together. I worked feverishly, in haste lest someone surprise me at my labours, though I knew that the people had shunned the Peabody homestead for decades. And then, this done, I laboured alone to drag Asaph Peabody's coffin and its hellish contents to the pyre, just as, decades before, Asaph himself had done to Jedediah's coffin and what it had contained! Then I stood by, while the holocaust consumed coffin and contents, so that I alone heard the high shrill wail of rage which rose from the flames like the ghost of a scream.

All that night the diminishing ashes of that pyre still glowed. I saw it from the windows of the house.

And inside, I saw something else.

A black cat which came to the door of my quarters and leered wickedly in at me.

And I remembered the path through the marsh I had taken, the muddied footprints, the mud on my shoes. I remembered the scratch on my wrist, and the Black Book I had signed. Even as Asaph Peabody had signed it.

I turned to where the cat lurked in the shadows and called it gently. 'Balor!'

It came and sat on its haunches just inside the door.

I took my revolver from the drawer of my desk and deliberately shot it.

It kept right on regarding me. Not so much as a whisker twitched.

Balor. One of the lesser devils.

This, then, was the Peabody heritage. The house, the grounds, the woods – these were only the superficial, material aspects of the extra-dimensional angles in the hidden room, the path through the marsh to the coven, the signatures in the Black Book. . . .

Who, I wonder, after I am dead, if I am buried as the others were, will turn me over?